I0460239

Miss Humbug

by Marnie L. Pehrson

Miss Humbug

by Marnie L. Pehrson

www.MissHumbug.com
www.MarniePehrson.com
www.CleanRomanceClub.com

Published by CES BUSINESS CONSULTANTS
© Copyright 2008 by Marnie L. Pehrson,
All Rights Reserved

The contents of this book may not be reproduced in any part or by any means without the written consent of the author.

First Printed Edition 2008
Printed in the United States of America
ISBN 0-9676162-6-3
Library of Congress Control Number: 2007908367

All character names and personalities in this work of fiction are entirely fictional, created solely in the imagination of the author. Any resemblance to any person living or dead is purely coincidental.

*To those who strive to live each day
with the Spirit of Christmas
in their hearts . . .*

December 16th

"Merry Christmas, Ms. Houston," the elderly doorman tipped his hat as he opened the glass door to the office complex.

"Good morning," Elaina Houston waved her gloved hand and brushed past him. She headed straight for the elevator and pressed the up button. The toe of her black stilettos impatiently tapped the green marble floor as she waited. She removed her gloves and put them in her coat pockets. After forty seconds, she released a heavy sigh and thrust her hand to her hip. Elaina's immaculate burgundy nails tapped against her black wool overcoat. Her eyes darted to the stair entrance and then down at her high heels.

Just as she decided that the stairs wouldn't be such a great idea, the elevator dinged and the door opened. She tossed her hand with an impatient flair and then hurried inside, carrying her leather briefcase as three people stepped off and four others followed her. Her index finger pressed 15 and both hands clasped the handle of the briefcase in front of her. The elevator stopped on nearly every floor between the first and the

15th, letting people off and others on. By the time they reached the tenth floor, Elaina checked her watch and released an irritated sigh – five 'til nine. She should be in her office right now.

She was so preoccupied with the time that she didn't notice Nick Aimes, the tall, strapping heartthrob of Mullins and Mullrooney Enterprises. Every woman in the office practically threw herself at the blonde-haired, blue-eyed Southerner. Born and bred near Nashville, Tennessee, his mother had evidently spent quite a bit of time training her son in the proper use of Ma'ams and Sir's and how to open doors and hail taxies for the fairer sex in such a way that even the most hardened New York City feminist could not be offended. He was quite a novelty in the mile-a-minute New York City life. The only woman who never gave him the time of day was Elaina Houston, Vice President of Marketing.

Elaina was as hard as those long burgundy nails of hers. For her, everything was about business. Her co-workers joked about her when she wasn't around. They wondered if she even slept. If she did, her dreams were probably about spreadsheets and marketing strategies. More likely she plugged into a recharging station at night like a Borg from *Star Trek*.

Nick smiled as he studied Elaina, his eyes traveling from her ash blonde hair pulled back in an immaculate bun to her professional business suit. He pictured her with wires coming out of her beautiful body connecting her to the collective consciousness of the Borg. The humor faded from his lips, replaced by a sad expression. She was really quite pitiful – cool and aloof most of the time. The only emotions she seemed to possess were irritation and impatience. As far as he could tell she had no family, no one who loved her, and no one to love. "Ice Woman" was what Charlie in packaging called her. Of course, Charlie was a relentless flirt and Nick had warned him he was wasting his energy pursuing Elaina. Nick remembered the time Charlie finally got up the nerve to ask her to dinner; Elaina shot him down cold.

"Thank you, No," was her frigid reply. If he'd been a telemarketer she would have replaced the receiver coolly before he got out his first, "But…" Instead she clapped her heels across the granite floor, entered her office and shut the door. She left Charlie with the proverbial tail caught between his legs.

If friendly Charlie couldn't pull off a dinner invitation with Elaina, no one else stood a chance. So no one else tried. That was two years ago and no one had attempted an invitation since. Even the females who tried to befriend Elaina found themselves pushed away.

Elaina glanced up at the floor indicator and noticed Nick staring at her. What was that expression on his face? Pity? The corners of his lips turned up and he nodded his head in a friendly gesture. The pity was still there though. She'd have none of it – neither his nor anyone else's. She made no attempt to return the acknowledgement, but turned her aloof gaze back to see that the elevator had now reached her floor. The doors opened and she rushed out, her stilettos clapping across the floor toward her office.

Nick exited after her, watched her for several moments, and then turned in the opposite direction toward his own office. He passed several people in the hall on his way.

"Good morning, Mr. Aimes," a tall redheaded secretary greeted him from her cubicle.

"Good morning, Melissa!" He gave her a cheery nod, "Merry Christmas!"

"Merry Christmas!" greeted several other office workers as they milled around the water cooler.

Elaina shut her office door and set her briefcase down on her desk, opened it and pulled out a memory stick containing the presentation she'd worked on last night at home. She walked over to the window to her office that looked out over the rows of cubicles. A glittering Christmas tree laden with gold, silver and red ornaments stood in the center. Cubicles encircled it as if everyone were gathered around some sort of shrine.

"Christmas," she gritted her teeth. *It won't be over soon enough for me. They're all useless at this time of year. Can't get a thing out of them*, she thought to herself. *All they do is watch the clock, waiting for the moment they can leave and go waste more of their money on presents, parties, and decorations.*

From a marketing standpoint, she had to admit that nothing was so ingenious as to have millions of people go out automatically every November and December and spend money they don't have on things they don't need. She wished she'd thought of it herself. As a matter of fact, she wished she owned a credit card company. Those people were the ones making a killing! Instead she worked for Mullins and Mullrooney. Those two had been in business since the day they graduated Harvard. They were the two most soft-hearted venture capitalists on the planet – investing in everything from innovative computer gadgets to the latest leak-guard diaper. Any inventor who thought he had the next best thing since the invention of the PC traipsed through

Mullins and Mullrooney Enterprises, pitching their wares.

It was Elaina's job to figure out how to market the stuff. Sometimes she had her job cut out for her because, personally, she couldn't see why anyone would buy the junk – no matter how Charlie from packaging wrapped it or Nick from development improved upon the design. The fact was, that Mr. Mullins and Mr. Mullrooney felt it their God-ordained obligation to help every poor dreamer they encountered. Because their hearts were bigger than their brains, the company didn't thrive the way Elaina knew it could.

"If I were in charge, things would be a lot different around here, that's for sure," she muttered under her breath. The first thing to go would be that stupid tree. She closed the shades so she wouldn't have to see the insufferable symbol of holiday cheer.

She sat down at her desk and went to work on her computer. She looked up when she heard a knock at the door.

"Come," she answered.

"Ms. Houston, here are the figures from Development and Packaging on that new diaper bag with the built-in bottle warmer," Angela laid a stack of papers on Elaina's desk.

"When will those guys ever learn to use e-mail and just shoot over the files?" Elaina asked her secretary.

Angela shrugged, "I believe it's because Mr. Mullins and Mr. Mullrooney like hard copies."

"But *I* don't like hard copies. They're a waste of paper and time. I just have to ask for the files anyway in order to perform my calculations."

"Yes, Ms. Houston. I'll pass along your suggestion again."

"Please do that. They don't seem to read my e-mails."

Angela nodded and left the room, mumbling something under her breath that Elaina didn't quite catch.

~*~

At 4:45 p.m., Elaina checked her e-mail and clicked the headline of the company-wide memo.

"Effective now through Christmas, everyone must vacate the building by 5:15 p.m. Go home and enjoy your families and the holiday season!

Merry Christmas!

*Mr. Roger Mullrooney
and Mr. Harry Mullins"*

"Good grief!" Elaina rolled her eyes. "How do they expect to run a profitable business with this kind of nonsense? Oh – right – I forgot – they aren't in it for profit," came her sarcastic quip. "Our mission statement is to 'make the little guys' dreams come true,'" she sneered with another roll of her eyes, talking to herself as she so often did.

She spent the last few minutes e-mailing work home to herself. If they wouldn't let her use her office, she'd just have to finish her work at home. Someone had to keep them from running the business into the ground.

The elevators overflowed with people following orders to vacate the building. Elaina managed to find a spot in the group taking the second elevator.

The crowd of people closed in around her. Elaina began to feel smothered as with each new floor the elevator picked up new people. Elaina took a deep breath, attempting to control her frustration. What was that tantalizing smell? It had to be the best smelling men's cologne on the planet. Why don't we represent the inventors of that stuff? She looked around to see who smelled so wonderful and found the source beside her. Nick Aimes' eyes followed the numbers – 12, 11, 10. He stood close – incredibly close. Her eyes darted back toward the door. Why was her heart beating so fast? Claustrophobia – that's it – crammed in this dinky elevator with so many people. She inhaled again.

Dang! He smells good!

The elevator stopped again, letting two more people on. As they nudged their way in, a woman in heels lost her balance and fell backwards, sending the others with a domino effect toward Elaina. Nick lunged forward and knocked Elaina off balance. He reached out his left hand to brace himself against the wall of the elevator and his other went around her waist. He pulled her toward him in one strong tug to prevent her from falling.

People shoved them so far over that now Elaina's back pressed against the wall of the elevator, Nick's arm still encircled her waist and his pale blue eyes caught hers as his left arm still braced against the wall over her head. His muscular form stood a full foot taller than her and as her eyes caught his, her heart hammered. She completely forgot to breathe. She could even feel a flush rising to her cheeks. He was smiling now – those darn dimples and his thick, smooth Tennessee accent was apologizing and asking her if she was okay.

Nick watched Elaina nod, indicating she was all right, then felt an elbow jab into his back, causing him to move even closer to her until their faces were only inches apart. She may be cool as a cucumber, but she was beautiful. A wisp of her ash blonde hair escaped from her careful bun, and he could see the struggle in her emerald eyes – wanting to maintain her cool exterior, but there was something else. His gaze dropped to her heart-shaped mouth.

Soon, the group in the elevator managed to right themselves, but Nick still leaned over her with his arm around her waist. Elaina forced her eyes from his, studying his engaging smile. It was a different one than he usually wore when he looked at her. There wasn't the usual pity. He was interested in her! For a fleeting second, Elaina felt flattered, but the emotion vanished as quickly as it arrived. Nonsense! She didn't have time for a messy office romance!

"Excuse me," she moved to escape his presence, but there wasn't much of anywhere to go.

Elaina deduced that Nick had come to his senses and realized he was hovering over the Ice Woman because he excused himself, released her, and turned to the door. They both stepped off the elevator on the first floor. Nick buttoned the top buttons of his khaki wool overcoat, tightened his red Christmas scarf around his neck and accompanied her to the front door.

The doorman opened the glass door, and Nick gestured for Elaina to go first.

"Merry Christmas, Elaina," Nick waved as she started left and he went right.

"Good night," she replied as she continued on her way, her heels clicking against the pavement.

~*~

Elaina opened the door to her spacious third floor apartment. She stepped onto the Mexican ceramic tile, then shut and locked her door. She walked around the black leather couch and reached for the remote lying on the glass coffee table. Flipping on the news, she only gave the flat panel television a glance. She stepped around a black recliner and headed toward the spare bedroom that she'd turned into an office. Elaina set her briefcase on her immaculate desk and passed the built-in bookshelves where every major business book and even a few obscure ones made their home.

She hit the switch on her computer and crossed the hall to her tidy bedroom where she kicked off her heels, hung up her coat and business suit and slipped into a pair of sweat pants and a sweatshirt. Sitting on the bed, she tugged on her gym socks. Elaina let down her ash-blonde hair from its bun and tied it back in a ponytail. Upon re-entering the living room, she changed the channel from the news to Food TV. Cooking was the only luxury Elaina afforded herself. She spent a few hours each night watching Food TV and experimenting in her kitchen. She crossed to the steel-clad refrigerator and pulled out the required ingredients that Tyler Florence indicated. She'd been to his web site ahead of time and purchased everything she needed for the salmon and risotto dish he prepared. Elaina followed along as if he were her own private instructor.

The chef was cute. He reminded her of Nick. Nick – the thought of him made her chop the carrots even finer and more furiously than Tyler Florence indicated. She could feel his arm around her again — see those pale blue eyes of his staring into hers. She could even feel the heat of her blush rising in her cheeks. If her heart were a block of ice, Nick raised the temperature enough to turn it to slush. No good could come of it. She stirred the risotto and then switched to sautéing her glazed carrots while her salmon broiled in the oven.

Instead of sitting at the kitchen table to waste more time with her thoughts of Nick, she carried her food to the office and pulled down the files she'd e-mailed herself from work. Work – that's all that mattered. Everything else was nonsense

– an utter waste of time. A business failure might bruise her ego or her pocketbook, but it couldn't crush her heart.

Elaina worked until around nine and then went back to the living room and flipped channels. *It's A Wonderful Life* – right! *Miracle on 34th Street* – Not! *Christmas Vacation* – Stupid! *Rudolph the Red-Nose Reindeer* – No Claymation - never! At length, she settled upon a documentary on the History Channel. Before long, she'd drifted off to sleep.

A few hours later, she awakened to the sound of Nat King Cole's Christmas song playing on a commercial. *"Chestnuts roasting on an open fire, Jack Frost nipping at your nose…"* sent Elaina's mind back through time, the memory as vivid as yesterday. It was Christmas of her twelfth year. She descended the garland-covered banister and glanced at her little brothers watching Claymation Christmas shows in the living room. She glanced toward the kitchen where Aunt Vicky was just taking a rum cake from the oven. Elaina smiled thinking of Vicky's earlier frantic state as her aunt nearly caught the kitchen on fire using too much rum at the wrong time.

Elaina approached the Christmas tree and reached for a miniature Santa. Moving him around the fuzzy tinsel rope as if it was a road in a Christmas village, she made Santa stop by to gather Christmas lists from Rudolf, Frosty, the angels, and the elves, before making his way back home to Mrs. Claus at the North Pole.

As Nat King Cole's Christmas song played on the stereo the doorbell rang, In a rush of excitement Elaina ran to the door to greet her cousins whom her parents had gone to pick up at the airport. But it wasn't her cousins. Two towering men in uniform stood at the door with a solemn expression. The house smelled a little like burnt rum and she would never forget that smell as long as she lived or Nat King Cole's voice as the men in uniform told her Aunt that Elaina's parents had been in a car accident. As Aunt Vicky slid to the floor, Elaina heard high-pitched screaming and realized it was herself.

The full suffocating reality of it slammed down on her like a cold iron vise. Tears poured down Elaina's cheeks as she pictured herself standing between two coffins – her mother on her right and her father on her left. Gone, both of them on Christmas Eve!

Elaina sat upright on the couch, hot tears streaming down her cheeks and cold beads of sweat dotting her neck, face and back. She ran to the bathroom, splashed cold water on her face and snubbed back the tears of a grieving twelve-year-old. She despised Christmas! Every year these horrid memories returned and grew worse each day leading up to that agonizing anniversary. Each year, she tried to steel herself against it, hardening her emotions, shutting out anyone or anything that might soften the chunk of ice in which she'd encased her broken heart. It never seemed to help. It only grew worse.

"What I wouldn't give to see mom and dad just one more time," she wished as she flipped off the bathroom light and went to the living room to turn off the television. She settled into bed with a business book. Business was the only thing that would drown out the hurt. Her only remedy was to wrap her mind around figures, formulae and marketing strategies in a world that made sense, a world she could predict. That was her only solace.

The howling winter wind blew through the open window, waking Elaina from her sleep. She moved the book from her chest and laid it on the night table beside her and noted the time – 3:00 a.m. Her eyes went next to the billowing curtains which let in the cold night air. She hadn't left the window open! Her heartbeat accelerated and she reached for a ball bat that she kept beside her bed. Creeping from beneath her covers, she approached the window, holding the bat in the air, ready to whack an unwanted intruder. Seeing no one, she closed the window and latched it.

She flipped on a light and crept through the house, bat in hand, making sure she was alone. After checking every nook and cranny, she felt satisfied that no intruder had joined her and settled back into bed with the bat lying beside her.

Just as she pulled the covers about her neck, two people appeared at the foot of her bed. She grabbed the bat and sat up.

"Who are you? Get out of my apartment!" she exclaimed.

The two people looked at each other and then at her. They appeared to be conversing with one another, but she couldn't hear them.

She jumped up and stood on her bed, the bat raised and ready to strike. They stood motionless, simply watching her. Their mouths moved, but she couldn't hear their words. In utter terror, she reared back and swung the bat at the man, but it passed right through him and kept on going through the woman. They remained unfazed.

Recognition flooded her mind, and Elaina sank to her knees in front of the apparitions. She covered her eyes, thinking she'd lost her mind. After mustering her courage to look once more, she moved her fingers and peeked out. They were still there.

"Elaina, honey, we're sorry we frightened you," her mother spoke in that comforting tone she remembered from childhood.

"Yes, Puddin', we knew it would be a shock, but never imagined you'd feel compelled to hit us with a baseball bat," her father laughed. He always had a quirky sense of humor. "I see you still have quite a swing."

Her mother turned to her father and giggled.

"What are you doing here? I'm dreaming," she hopped off the bed and started pacing the room, "I'm dreaming and I just need to wake up." She left the room, turned on the bathroom light and splashed water on her face. Returning to her bedroom, she found them facing her as she came through the door. She flipped on the light thinking that would make them leave, but it didn't. The light only helped her see them more clearly.

Her mother wore a flowing white dress, gathered at the waist with a belt. Her father wore a white suit. A soft glow surrounded them.

"We realize it's a shock, but we only have a little bit of time, and it's important that you listen to us."

Elaina flopped down on a chair and held her head in her hands, rubbing her eyes, looking up and rubbing her eyes again, trying to shake the vision.

"You're really here?" she finally started to come to grips with the reality of the situation.

"Yes, we're really here, and you need to listen to us. We've only been granted a little bit of time to warn you," her father explained.

"Warn me?"

"Yes, Puddin'," her mother answered.

"About what?"

"Unless you make some changes in your life, you won't live to see another Christmas," her father blurted as if saying it fast would somehow cushion the blow.

"What do you mean, I won't see another Christmas?"

"Over the next week, you must either capture the Spirit of Christmas or you will not live to see another December 25th. Your very life depends upon it."

"Catch the Spirit of Christmas? You've got to be kidding! I hate Christmas! You died on Christmas Eve. Who would expect me to like Christmas – much less catch the spirit of it?" she exclaimed, rising from her chair.

"We realize that it has been very difficult for you, Elaina, but our death was never supposed to turn you into this," her mother waved her hand as if to indicate that Elaina were a complete and utter mess. "You are no longer living the life you were born to live. Either you get back on track with the life God has for you, or your life on earth must end."

Bitterness rose within her and poured out in the tone of her voice, "Well, God should have thought about that, shouldn't he? He should have known what it would do to a 12-year-old to lose both of her parents on Christmas Eve!"

"Your brothers have adjusted to it, Elaina. But you – you've isolated yourself. You're cold, hardened and alone. You're miserable, Puddin', can't you see that?" her father explained.

"Sure, throw Chuck and Eric up to me. Chuck with the beautiful wife and three kids in Morristown and Eric with his perfect Southern belle homemaker and five kids in Atlanta! They were little when you were killed. They barely even remember you. They don't know what they've missed out on! I do – I still remember what it felt like to have you sing me to sleep at night and read me stories! I still remember you cheering me on at my softball games and coming to my school plays!" Tears were streaming down her cheeks now. She wouldn't have thought that spirits could cry, but even her parents seemed to have shimmering moisture in their eyes.

"We're so sorry, honey, but you must know that our leaving was for the best. It was part of God's plan for us and for you children," her mother soothed.

"God's plan? God's plan stinks! I want nothing to do with it!" she bellowed.

"Shhh- Don't say such things," her father scolded. "You aren't seeing the big picture."

"Then explain it to me, Dad! What's the big picture here? Why was it in my best interest to lose my parents at twelve?" she countered.

"It made you the strong, independent woman you are," her father answered.

"But you just said that I'm not the person I'm supposed to be! You're talking in circles!"

Her mother answered in a quiet, soothing voice, "As a result of our deaths, you have characteristics that you need for your purpose in life, but you've closed yourself off. There are people you are supposed to help that you aren't helping. There are people that you are supposed to love that you aren't loving. Your life is off course. You have lost your purpose."

"We don't have time for this," her father's head jerked toward her mother as if he'd heard a warning bell letting them know their time was almost up.

He continued, "Now open your heart for a minute and listen to us, Elaina. You have seven days to capture the Spirit of Christmas – to learn to live a Christ-like life. Your very existence depends upon it. Three times in the next seven days death will knock at your door. Live as you were born to live, and you will escape unscathed.

Live this cold, hardened life you have chosen, and you will die."

"But I don't know how to live a Christ-like life!" she begged. "I wouldn't even know where to begin! I haven't stepped in a church in years!"

Elaina watched as her mother floated from the room into her office and back again carrying a book. Her mother opened the book to its center and set it on the bed.

"Start reading there," her mother pointed. "Be observant. God's messages are all around you. They could be anywhere - on anything – most of them you'll find in that book. When they come, you will feel it in your heart – that they're from God. Listen and act accordingly."

"But" Elaina began to protest, but they began to fade from view. "Don't go!" she pleaded.

"We love you, Puddin'. No matter what happens, we will always love you," they assured in unison as they faded from sight.

Elaina sank to the floor, her head in her hands and tears flooding from her eyes.

When she finally regained control, she crossed to the bed and found her mother's old Bible opened to Matthew chapter 1. She lifted the book, pulled back the covers, lay down and began to read.

As Elaina read Matthew, she kept looking for clues for living a Christ-like life. She found it quite ironic that she, a person who cared nothing about Christmas or other people for that matter, was now frantically scouring through a Bible searching for ways to live the Spirit of Christmas! Reading a Bible of all things!

It was all too overwhelming. Love your enemies, serve others, turn the other cheek, give of yourself, judge not, and be merciful. If all of this was what she should have been doing with her life then there was little wonder her parents insisted she was off track. She was like that salt that had lost its savor and was henceforth good for nothing but to be cast out and trodden under the foot of men. Actually, she'd be snuffed out of existence – her very life depended upon her figuring out how to live like Jesus lived.

Most of all she wondered how she could be a city set on a hill and not let her right hand know what her left was doing. How do you shine without letting anyone know you're shining? How do you gain your life by losing it? How do you turn the other cheek, go the extra mile and not become a doormat that no one respects? How do you put God first, instead of your work, and still expect to have food, clothing and raiment? There were too many paradoxes in His teachings. How was she supposed to understand it all, much less assimilate it in one week – less than one week!

She was too tired to think about it now. She set the book aside, turned off the lamp and went to sleep.

December 17th

Elaina's dreams were filled with the scenes she'd read – a baby born in Bethlehem, the little family fleeing to Egypt to escape Herod's edict, Jesus being baptized of John, being tempted in the wilderness and performing miracle after miracle. He healed the sick, made the lame walk, cleansed the lepers, gave the blind their sight, and fed the five thousand.

In those fitful moments between dreams and consciousness a single phrase ran through her mind "The greatest gift is the gift of self." It was a male voice inside her head. Her subconscious argued, *But I've got nothing inside myself worth giving!* Again, the voice came more insistent, "The greatest gift is the gift of self." The scene of Jesus feeding the five thousand flashed across her mind and the phrase repeated itself a third time.

Elaina bolted upright. She suddenly knew what she had to do – at least where she could start. She flung back her green down comforter, ran to the kitchen, and pulled several assorted flavors of chocolate chips from her pantry, some marshmallow cream, sweetened condensed milk and vanilla. Yes, she had everything. At this time of year, all the stores put the ingredients for candy and desserts on sale, and Elaina's sweet tooth couldn't resist stocking up. She was glad she'd done so again this year.

How much time did she have? She noted the microwave clock as six a.m. She believed, if she hurried, she'd have just enough time to whip up a monster batch of fudge, take a shower, dress and run to the store for a few items she'd need.

Her mind flashed back to baking with her mother years earlier. Her mother would turn on Christmas music, sing and dance along as she and the kids made holiday goodies. But, Elaina didn't own a single Christmas CD. She grabbed the remote, flipped on the television and scoured the channels for that music station she'd seen the other day. Yes! There it was - the holiday music channel. A piano and guitar rendition of "What Child Is This?" played through the speakers.

Elaina made a double batch of fudge and spread it into pans to cool, then hopped in the shower. After dressing, she cut the fudge into pieces, put it in a large container and covered it. She grabbed her briefcase and fled out the door, with her briefcase in one hand and the fudge in the other.

On wintry mornings like this, she was glad her apartment complex had a covered parking garage. She tossed her briefcase in the back seat of her *champagne*-tinted Camry, put the fudge in the passenger seat, and started the engine. While the car heated, Elaina scanned for a Christmas station. The music brought with it such an odd range of emotions and memories. She'd laugh one minute with a fond remembrance and cry the next.

By the time she reached the store, blew her nose, and dried her eyes, she decided perhaps she should ease herself into Christmas music in smaller doses. She parked the car and hurried toward the automatic doors. She'd never bought them before, but she knew she'd seen them the other day in passing. Yes! There they were - little white candy boxes with a red ribbon design printed on the box – perfect for fudge. She grabbed a roll of wax paper, a box of Christmas cards, a roll of tape and a huge Christmas bag; then headed for the checkout counter.

In the car, Elaina assembled the Christmas boxes, lined them with wax paper, filled them with fudge and secured them with a strip of tape. By the time she was done, she had filled the large Christmas bag three-quarters from the top. That would be plenty for everyone, she surmised.

"Merry Christmas, Ms. Houston," the doorman greeted.

"Merry Christmas, Mr. Dunkin!" she chimed the merry greeting. She reached in her bag, pulled out a box of fudge and handed it to him.

"For me?" he asked in surprise, pointing to his chest.

"For you, yes. Merry Christmas!" she smiled.

His eyes widened in shock as he stared at her and then his disbelief transformed into a smile. "Thank you, Ms. Houston," he replied taking the box.

"Oh, just call me Elaina," she patted his arm.

The elderly gentleman looked down at her hand on his arm and then looked up into her face. "Then call me Darryl, Miss – Elaina."

"Gotta run, Darryl. Merry Christmas!" she waved as she headed for the elevator with her briefcase and bag.

This time, she didn't even notice that the elevator took several minutes to arrive. She was too busy mentally counting the number of people in her office and calculating whether she had enough fudge for everyone.

Three women from her office joined her outside the elevator door and eyed the bright and cheery Christmas bag. One woman leaned over to the lady beside her and whispered into her hair, "Someone gave her a gift?"

Both women raised their eyebrows in disbelief.

When Elaina reached the fifteenth floor at eight-forty, she walked around leaving boxes of fudge at each cubicle.

"Merry Christmas!" she'd say as she passed an occupied desk and placed a box of fudge in front of the person. Some people were so dumbfounded by the gesture that they became speechless or choked out a weak Merry Christmas in return. She placed boxes on the empty desks and kept moving until all twenty-two on her floor had a box of fudge. When she'd completed her task, she went to her office, pulled out one of the Christmas cards she'd purchased for those with whom she worked most closely. She signed it, put Angela's name on the outside and placed it along with a box of fudge on her secretary's desk.

Without even taking the time to start her computer, she continued to sign cards and label them with names. She placed them in the gift bag with the fudge and then deciding she'd covered every base, she started her computer to begin her work day.

"Ms. Houston, wow, thank you for the fudge! It's delicious!" Angela popped her head into Elaina's office.

"You're welcome, Angela. I'm glad you enjoyed it."

"Did you make this?" Angela's eyes were filled with wonder as she held up a half-eaten piece of chocolate confection.

"This morning," Elaina nodded.

"It's delicious! Thank you so much!" Angela ate the remainder.

"Thank you. Merry Christmas!" Elaina smiled, and she realized at that moment that she meant what she said. She wasn't going through motions trying to force herself to say "Merry Christmas" – two words she hadn't uttered in twelve years. She really meant them. Just taking the time to think of others and do some small simple gesture had changed her somehow. It was hardly feeding the five thousand, but it had shifted something in her attitude.

Angela shook her head in shock. The secretary started to leave but remembered something, "Oh, just a reminder, there's a staff meeting at 9:30 and you have lunch with the development team."

"Thank you, Angela," Elaina nodded.

"Do you need me to do anything for you? Get you a cup of coffee?"

Elaina rose from her chair and headed for the door. "Actually, I'm in the mood for some hot chocolate this morning. I'll get it myself. Would you like a cup?"

Angela looked at her boss as if a benevolent alien had taken possession of her body. "That sounds great. Are you sure you don't want me to get it?"

"Go enjoy your fudge," Elaina patted Angela's arm and the secretary stared at the spot in disbelief as Elaina's heels clicked toward the break room.

"What's gotten into her?" an amazed woman stepped toward Angela.

"I have no idea, but it's something good! Elaina Houston never touches anyone, much less smiles and distributes fudge!" Angela's eyes widened and her head shook in confusion.

Elaina got to the staff room early and placed nine boxes of fudge and a matching number of Christmas cards around the oval boardroom table. She'd just set down the last two when Nick from Development followed by three others entered the room. The people walked around the table and found their seats by locating the cards with their names on them. Without realizing it, Elaina had put Nick's card in the seat next to the only chair left with no card – her chair!

She glanced up at Nick standing beside her, then diverted her eyes at the table. *Good grief!*

He's going to think I planned it this way! But she hadn't! They just landed in that order.

Everyone took their seats and Mr. Mullins called the meeting to order, thanked Elaina for the gifts and suggested everyone enjoy their fudge as they worked. Normally, Elaina perceived the frivolity of the Mullins and Mullrooney staff meetings as an utter waste of time, but not today. She actually enjoyed it, laughed at Mr. Mullrooney's silly jokes and exchanged smiles with her co-workers. She even found that the light-heartedness had loosened up her brainstorming, and she threw out a couple wonderful ideas that Mr. Mullins insisted they act upon.

Nick couldn't believe that smile. Where had it been hiding for the last four years? If his heart had been secretly attracted to Elaina before this, now it had come out of the closet with full blown admission! Dimples – the woman had dimples! How could someone hide dimples for four years? There was something else different about her. Before when he looked into Elaina's eyes, the lights were off and nobody was home, but something had changed. Not only were there inhabitants, but a festive dinner party carried on inside! Something had happened to her, and Nick wanted to hear the full story.

After the meeting, Nick stopped Elaina at the door, "Are we still on for lunch today?"

"Right, you, Stacy and I are supposed to coordinate our efforts on the diaper bag warmer," she answered, a slight tremor in her voice. "Where is Stacy anyway?" Elaina's eyes turned to stare at the card and fudge that still remained untouched in front of an empty seat.

"Stacy got a call from her son's school, and she had to pick him up. She couldn't find a sitter on such short notice and probably won't be coming back for the rest of the day," Nick replied.

"Do we need to reschedule for tomorrow then?" Elaina suggested, discretely wiping her palms on her skirt.

"No, I think we need to get started on this. Stacy's left me her ideas. We can just go over them ourselves. I'll stop by your office around noon, and we'll go from there," Nick nodded and left.

Elaina spent the rest of the morning clicking away on her computer buried in facts, figures and projections.

"Come on in," she answered the rap on her door without turning her head away from the monitor.

"You ready to go?" It was Nick's voice. Her palms began to perspire and her heart to race. What had gotten into her? Sure, there had been an underlying tension between her and Nick, but it had never affected her this way. She deduced that it must be all the emotion she'd let herself experience so suddenly – the Christmas music, the old memories – it was all making her a little disoriented. Soon she'd adjust, and she'd be back in control again - none of this profuse hand-sweating and heart palpitations.

She took a deep breath, wiped her hands on a tissue and turned around, "Sure, we can go now. Just let me save what I'm working on."

She turned off her monitor, grabbed her briefcase and followed Nick out the door.

"Do you feel like Italian, Mexican or Chinese?" he asked as they made their way to the elevator.

"All of it sounds good to me. You pick," she suggested.

"All right, then, I know a quiet little Mexican restaurant where we can go over the project," he pressed the elevator button.

Nick started explaining the new technology they'd designed for the baby-bottle warmer. She listened, but her mind was too busy thinking about how straight and white his teeth were. He must have had braces.

"We can take my car, if you want," Nick suggested as he put out his hand to hold the elevator door, letting her step off.

When they reached his Explorer in the staff parking lot, he opened the door for her and helped her climb into the passenger side. She made a mental note to herself to wear lower heels the next time she had a lunch meeting with Nick.

He climbed in, and lowered the volume on the Christmas choir CD he had playing in his stereo. She never would have pegged Nick as a Mormon Tabernacle Choir lover.

They continued to talk business on their way to the restaurant, and Elaina began to relax a little and feel more herself. Business was her comfort zone. She reassured herself that she didn't need to feel anxious. She could talk business from now until doomsday.

Before Elaina could figure out how to open the Explorer door, Nick was outside, helping her exit the vehicle.

"You're definitely the Southern boy, aren't you?" she chuckled.

"Yeah, I guess I haven't lost my accent yet," he smiled.

"No, I was referring to the door opening," she noted.

"Does that offend you?" he asked with sincere concern.

"Oh, no," she shrugged. "It's just unusual in this city."

"Well, it's awfully hard to undo what my Mama taught me," he said as he threw himself into his best Tennessee accent, and she couldn't hold back a chuckle. He gave her an odd look, and she suspected that he wasn't use to hearing her laugh. She was so out of practice, she wondered if her laugh sounded strange.

As they sat down to lunch, Nick looked across the table at her and his expression grew more serious, "You're different."

"What?" she asked.

"There's something different about you," he stated.

Elaina shrugged, "What do you mean by different? Good different or bad different?"

"You're happy. You've got a light in your eyes that wasn't there before. What's going on with you?"

Elaina's eyebrows rose, "You're rather direct this afternoon, aren't you?"

"I'm sorry, I guess that was a bit forward of me," he gave an apologetic gesture of his hands. "You don't have to answer that."

"Good, 'cause I don't know how to answer the question," she shrugged. What was she going to say? My deceased parents appeared to me last night and told me to read my mother's old Bible, and I woke up this morning with an incredible urge to feed the five thousand with fudge?

"So what are you doing this Christmas? Anything special?" he asked, leaning his elbows on the table.

How did we shift into personal gear? she wondered.

"I don't have any plans yet. I usually work through the holidays. But this year, I don't know. Doesn't seem like the right thing to do," she put her finger to her lips mulling more to herself than speaking to Nick.

Realizing she'd drifted off into her own thoughts, she caught herself and looked at him, "What are you doing?"

"I usually go home to Tennessee for Christmas, but this year my parents are on a mission in the Ukraine, and my brothers and sisters are spread out with their families all over the country. So I guess I'm just hanging out at my apartment."

"You should come over, I'll make you some turkey and dressing from the recipe I saw on Food 911," she replied, then clamped her mouth shut. Elaina's eyes widened. Did she just invite Nick to eat Christmas dinner with her? Where did that come from?

"Are you serious?" he asked, with raised eyebrows.

Her heart began to pound. "Well, sure, since neither of us have anywhere else better to go."

She'd stuck her toe in the water; she may as well drown herself.

"Thank you, I might take you up on that," he smiled. "I just have to check on one thing first. Can I let you know by Wednesday?"

"Sure," she nodded. "Now . . . about this bottle warmer . . . " She shifted the conversation back to business where it stayed throughout the remainder of the meal and the drive back to the office.

When they stepped off the elevator on the fifteenth floor, Nick put his hand on her arm, "I'll let you know about Christmas by Wednesday. Thanks for the offer."

"Sure," she nodded. She turned left and went to her office. Nick turned right to go to his.

On her drive home from work, Elaina decided to stop at the grocery store for a few things. The store was so busy from after-work shoppers that she had to park at the end of the parking lot near the road. She went inside and purchased the items she needed and then pushed the grocery cart out the door and toward her car. She unlocked her car and put her groceries into the trunk. It had started raining while she shopped, and the precipitation drizzled onto her hair, face and shoulders, sending cold shivers over her body.

She pushed the cart into an empty parking space beside her own to leave it there, but then she thought better of it. Somebody else could use this parking space, not to mention the poor kid who would have to gather up carts in the rain.

She locked her car door and pushed the cart across the parking lot to the nearest repository. Just as she let the cart go, she heard screeching tires and a metallic grinding crash. Her head turned toward the commotion where, back across the parking lot, a car had slid off the road and crushed in the driver's side of her Camry!

Her heart raced and she ran across the parking lot to her car. Her driver's side was completely caved in. She swore and was fully prepared to chew out the driver when she looked inside to see a young teenager with blood streaming down her face. Elaina yanked open the girl's door and squatted down so that she was eyelevel with the her.

"Are you all right?" she asked.

Tears mingled with the blood on the girl's cheeks. "I'm so sorry! I slid out of control! Is that your car?"

"Yes, but don't worry about it. Are you okay?"

The girl dabbed at the blood on her forehead and looked as if she were going to pass out.

Elaina pulled her cell phone and some tissue from her purse. She handed the girl the tissue to stop the bleeding and dialed 911 to report the accident.

Soon an ambulance and a police car arrived. The paramedics felt the girl would be all right, but they took her to the hospital for precautionary measures.

The lanky male officer handed Elaina her driver's license and registration, "You're lucky you weren't in your car when it hit, or you'd be dead right now."

Elaina turned pale as her father's voice echoed through her mind, "Three times in the next seven days death will knock at your door."

"Are you all right, Miss?" the officer asked. Elaina didn't reply, just stared at the wrecker towing away her Camry. "Can we give you a lift to a rental place?" He touched her arm.

Coming out of her thoughts, she said, "Oh, yes, could you please?"

Elaina sat in the back seat of the police car with her groceries, digesting the fact that if she'd been her usual self – too busy to put up a shopping cart – too thoughtless to think of anyone but herself – she'd be dead right now. An eerie shiver ran along her spine and for the first time since her parents' visit, the seriousness of her mortality hit her – and hit her hard. Next time she might not be so lucky! What if she missed some small and simple thing she should do for someone else and it cost her her life! Suddenly, it was all a lot more important than making fudge for co-workers!

It was well past dark by the time Elaina rented a car and neared her apartment. On the way there, she passed a church with a sign outside.

The message on the sign made her heart stop and her breath catch:

"Jesus knew that the significance of our service does not depend upon its scale."

December 18th

The somber reality of her mortality drove Elaina to her Bible again and even to her knees in prayer. It had been ages since she'd prayed with her parents, but somehow it came back to her. When she awoke Saturday morning the phrase that had stood out to her the evening before came wafting through her mind, "freely ye have received, freely give" (Matthew 10:8).

She had to admit that she had received many wonderful things in her life – a well-paying job, a pleasant work environment, a nice apartment with all the furnishings and luxuries of life she needed. Yet she couldn't think of anything she'd given anyone in years other than yesterday's fudge.

She took a relaxing shower, dressed and then stepped outside on her balcony to watch the snow fall. She captured a few flakes in her hand and then looked down into the alley below where a woman and her young teenage son huddled at the side of the building. The woman's fingers poked through her worn gloves and her son's shoes were falling apart. His jeans were torn.

Elaina grabbed her coat and purse, locked up her apartment and headed out the door. She hadn't even taken time to eat breakfast, but she knew she needed to act fast.

She jogged to her car and drove to the nearest superstore. She picked out two sets of gloves, two coats, two scarves, two thermal blankets, two warm hats, and several grocery items that wouldn't require cooking. Rather than guess at shoe and clothes sizes, she put a couple hundred dollars on a gift card and headed back toward home.

She hoped they were still there. She parked her car and carried the bags into the alley. Looking around, she was unable to find the mother and son. Just as she was about to give up and come back later, she spotted them huddled together by a dumpster.

"Hello," she said. The pair looked up at her, shivering. It was obvious they were surprised that someone like her would be talking to them.

Elaina held out the bags toward them, "Merry Christmas!"

The woman hesitated and then rose to her feet. Her son, not as timid as his mother, grabbed the bags.

"Slow down, Hakeem," the woman put a staying hand on her son's arm.

"It's all right. These things are for you," Elaina motioned for them to take the bags.

The woman's shaking fingertips took hold of one bag. She looked inside it and pulled out a down thigh-length coat. Her son reached for another bag and pulled out the coat Elaina had purchased for him.

"Are you kidding?" the boy's eyes lit up as he started rummaging through the bags.

"I don't know what to say," the woman stared at Elaina with grateful eyes.

"Oh, here," Elaina pulled the gift card from her purse along with some cash, "I didn't know what sizes you wore, so you can use this to pick out the clothes and shoes you want. You should be able to hale a taxi or catch a bus with the cash."

The boy put on the gloves and coat while his mother took the gift card.

"Thank you!" the woman smiled through her tears.

"I live on the third floor in apartment 304 if you need somewhere to crash," Elaina offered before she realized what she'd said.

"Oh we couldn't impose on you," the woman shook her head. "We stay at the shelter, but thank you for offering."

"But you must join me for Christmas dinner Saturday! I'm making a turkey with all the trimmings," Elaina smiled.

The woman just stared at her in shock.

"Remember, apartment 304, around six. My name is Elaina Houston."

"Roberta and Hakeem Baker," the woman extended her hand and Elaina shook it.

"Nice to meet you," Elaina smiled. There was a grateful twinkle in the woman's eyes. Elaina knew she hadn't made a mistake. Most people would have called her crazy for offering a total stranger a Christmas dinner, but deep down, Elaina knew she'd done the right thing.

She bid the two farewell as they exited the alley bundled warm in their new coats, gloves, and scarves.

"Thank you!" the boy called out to her once more and then shoved a granola bar into his mouth.

Elaina's smile spread from ear to ear. She'd never felt so good in all of her life.

December 19th

Elaina's alarm went off at 7:00 a.m. Sunday morning. She'd taken some time to get on the Internet the night before and found the church her mother and father belonged to when they were alive. Perhaps it was time for her to go back to church.

She'd found a building for her childhood denomination not five miles from her apartment with the meetings starting at nine. She hopped in the shower and got dressed in a nice skirt and sweater.

It was going to feel strange going back to church after so many years. Of course no one would know her. It wasn't the same building her parents had attended anyway – just the same denomination. She remembered enjoying church as a child, it was just when her parents died, she'd shut herself off from anything and everything that reminded her of them.

The old bitterness started to rise, and she shoved it aside. Still, she had to admit she was terrified. Attending church was a big step. At least no one would know her, and she could just say she was visiting from out of town or something so they wouldn't expect her to come again if she didn't like it.

She arrived a few minutes early and parked her rental car fairly close to the door. She'd learned from the Internet that there was a women's meeting first. But she had no idea what room they met in.

"Good morning!" two young men in suits and overcoats met her at the door, opening it wide for her to enter. The taller one introduced himself and his companion with a handshake.

"Good morning," she smiled, taking the shorter one's hand in greeting.

"Are you new?" they asked.

"I'm just visiting. Could you please point me in the right direction for the first meeting?" Elaina asked.

"Right down this hall and to the right."

Elaina thanked them and followed their directions. The women were friendly and introduced themselves, making her feel at home. She kept with the "I'm visiting" story in hopes they wouldn't ask too many questions, but by the time the meeting was over, Elaina volunteered that she had grown up as a member of their denomination but had not attended since her parents died twelve years ago.

The women invited her to another Wednesday night meeting the week after Christmas. She decided she just might attend.

One woman her age introduced herself as Miranda Reinhardt and took Elaina under her wing. She showed her to the adult Sunday school class. Elaina's heart stopped when the second she walked through the door of the room, the tall familiar form of Nick Aimes stood in front of her. He looked fabulous in his white shirt, tie and navy suit.

Nick took a double take and headed in her direction.

"Elaina! What are you doing here?" he took her hand in his.

"Just visiting," she responded.

"Are you a friend of Miranda's?" Nick's quizzical eyes darted to Miranda.

Elaina smiled, "No, I just came here today because I thought it was time I started going to church again. It's been years."

"Since your parents died, you said, right?" Miranda chimed in.

"Oh, I'm sorry. I didn't know your parents had passed away." Nick's concern seemed geniune..

"It was twelve years ago," Elaina waved her hand as if it were no big deal. She didn't feel like going into details.

"Well, it's about time we got started," Nick looked at his watch.

Miranda motioned for Elaina to follow her, and Elaina expected Nick to join them, but he didn't. Instead he stood at the front of the room, grabbed a piece of chalk and welcomed everyone to the class. He was the Sunday school teacher! She couldn't believe it, but then again she could – it explained a lot.

After welcoming Elaina and a few other visitors to the class, Nick asked someone to offer a prayer and began his lesson.

Elaina absorbed every word as if she were a ravenous homeless person who'd been offered a banquet meal in a cozy shelter. She felt warm and tingly all over. As wonderful as it was to have Nick for the instructor, she knew it wasn't him causing her to feel this way. It was more than that. The lesson struck a chord with her soul, and she wanted to learn all she could about the faith of her parents.

After the concluding prayer, Nick accompanied Elaina and Miranda to the next meeting where they sang songs and listened to speakers. Elaina joined in the Christmas carols. Every once in a while she caught Nick staring at her.

Elaina was a complete puzzle to Nick. How could the Ice Woman from work be sitting on the pew next to him singing Christmas carols in a loud and lovely voice? There was always something that drew him to her. He'd spent quite a bit of time worrying about her. He knew deep down she was a decent person. She never back-stabbed anyone, cheated or cut corners. She always did her best at whatever she set out to do. She had just been so closed off and alone – so emotionless and cold - even a little cruel at times and definitely impatient, but never dishonest or unethical. She'd often been the object of his nightly prayers.

Elaina was like some poor lost soul calling out for help without realizing she wanted or needed it. And now here she sat next to him, and he hadn't done a single thing to help her be there – other than praying for her. Nick couldn't help but realize that today he had not only witnessed an answer to prayer, but a modern miracle!

~*~

Settling back into her apartment, Elaina changed out of her skirt and slipped on a pair of jeans. She looked at the calendar. There were only five more days until Christmas Eve and two more near-death experiences to survive. As much as she felt she was doing the right things, she still couldn't shake the constant trepidation in knowing that death lurked at her doorstep. What if she forgot something?

The verse she'd read the night before came to mind, "God hath not given us the spirit of fear, but of power and of love and a sound mind."

She couldn't react out of fear. She had to do her best and hope that God would take care of the rest.

She spent the afternoon reading, pondering and taking a nap. After a light dinner, she settled in for the evening to watch, *It's a Wonderful Life*.

December 20th

"Mr. Mullins needs you to take the three o'clock shuttle to Boston to have dinner with the Langley's and discuss their project," Angela set a plane ticket on Elaina's desk.

"Really? Today?" Elaina's eyebrows rose and she felt a bit perturbed about the impossition.

"They're having a dinner meeting and they need a representative from Mullins and Mullrooney there."

"But I won't get out of my meeting with the Gilberts until after one. That's cutting it awfully close for a three o'clock flight!"

"I know, I told him that, but he insists you need to go."

"Great," Elaina shook her head with a frown.

"Sorry," Angela shrugged.

"Oh, it's not your fault. Just one of those things," Elaina offered a weak smile. Who did they think she was? Superwoman?

She grabbed the ticket, her briefcase and her coat so she wouldn't need to return to her office.

~*~

Elaina looked at her watch when she stepped out of the meeting. It was already quarter past one. She had one hour to get to the airport before she'd be unable to board. She kicked off her heels and carried them, running to the elevator.

She passed Nick in the hallway and heard him chuckle at her harried state.

She pressed the elevator button and called back to him, "Gotta catch the three o'clock shuttle to Boston!"

"Good luck!" he waved.

"Thanks! I'll need it." The elevator doors opened and she stepped inside. She replaced her shoes when she reached the bottom floor. Soon she was out on the sidewalk heading for the employee parking lot.

"Can you please help me?" Elaina registered a child's faint voice, but kept on going.

"Please?" the little girl begged.

Elaina looked over her shoulder at a small dark-haired child with tears streaming down her chubby cheeks.

Elaina glanced at her watch and then the words, *"Suffer the little children to come unto me for such is the kingdom of heaven"* entered her mind with clarity and force.

She stopped, squatted down and pulled a tissue from her pocket to dry the little girl's tears. "What's wrong sweetheart?"

"I lost my Mommy," the child replied.

"Oh my," Elaina looked around trying to find any motherly-looking women in the area, but saw only a sea of people in business suits. No one seemed to fit with the child.

"Where were you when you saw her last?"

"She took me to the drugstore. I stopped to play with the dolls and when I looked up she was gone. I looked all over the store, but couldn't find her. I came outside to look for Mommy, but I can't find her anywhere," the six-year-old snubbed back her tears.

"Where you in CVS Pharmacy? There's a CVS near here,"

"I think so," the girl sniffed.

"You've walked for several blocks! It'll be faster if we take my car," Elaina took the little girl's hand and started toward her vehicle. But the child wouldn't budge.

"What's wrong?"

"My Mommy told me never to get into cars with strangers," the little girl swung her head side-to-side.

Elaina hung her head in frustration, "Great!" She stared at her heels. She really needed to buy a pair of comfortable shoes if she was going to keep playing Good Samaritan.

"Then, will you walk with me?" Elaina asked.

"Uh-huh," the child nodded.

"All right, let's go," Elaina took her hand and hurried on, but then realized the child couldn't keep up the pace. She slowed her steps and they walked several blocks together. As they approached the drugstore, the automatic doors opened and they stepped inside.

Elaina led the girl to the customer service counter and explained the situation. The child's mother had indeed been searching for her. When she hadn't found her daughter in the store, she went to the customer service desk, left her cell phone number, and set out to search the streets.

The clerk called the number and the mother answered on the first ring.

Elaina bent down eye level with the little girl, "Okay, sweetie, your Mommy is on her way now, and I have a plane to catch. Stay here with this nice clerk until your Mommy comes back."

"Please don't leave me," the child's big brown eyes pleaded.

Elaina hung her head, took a deep breath and glanced at her watch. It was already a quarter until two. Maybe – just maybe she could make it if she left now. But the little girl looked so pitiful, she just couldn't leave her.

The grateful mother appeared within a few minutes, threw her arms around the child and thanked Elaina profusely for finding her. The little girl hugged Elaina's waist and she returned the gesture, waved goodbye and stepped outside.

Elaina decided to hail a taxi, but it hit red light after red light. By the time she entered the terminal, her flight was taxiing out to the runway. There wasn't another shuttle to Boston until seven – too late for the meeting.

"Oh well," she threw her hands into the air. "Maybe now they'll stop expecting me to be Superwoman!"

While sitting at a traffic light, she picked up her cell phone and called Angela but got her voice mail. She left a message asking her to tell Mr. Mullins that she had missed her flight and was on her way home.

It was nearly five when Elaina walked through her apartment door. She hung up her coat and went straight to her bedroom to change. While she slipped her sweatshirt over her head, the phone rang. She picked up the receiver.

"Miss Houston! Is that you?" Angela's voice sounded frantic.

"Yes."

"Oh, I'm so glad!" she released a heavy sigh.

"What's wrong, Angela?"

"I got your voice mail, and I just wanted to double check that you weren't on that flight," Angela sounded shaky.

"Why?"

"Have you not seen the news?" Angela asked. "Turn on the television. It's bound to be on. I saw it as a newsflash on the Web."

Elaina went to the television and turned on a network channel.

Angela's voice was flat and grave, "Shuttle flight 1204 to Boston crashed before it reached the airport. There were no survivors."

Elaina felt numb and sank onto a living room chair. She stared at the television screen, which displayed scenes from the wreckage. She lowered the phone from her ear and rested it in her lap, staring at the twisted metal and strewn luggage.

She couldn't believe it! "That little girl saved my life," she whispered to herself.

"Miss Houston, are you there?" Elaina could hear the faint sound of Angela's voice and lifted the phone back to her ear.

"How horrible!" Elaina choked back her emotions as silent tears trickled down her cheeks. "I could have been on that flight! All those poor people!"

"Mr. Aimes is here, Ms. Houston. He'd like to speak with you."

"Nick?" Elaina's eyebrows furrowed.

"Yes," Angela handed the phone to Nick.

"Elaina, I'm so glad you weren't on that flight!" he exclaimed.

"You and me both," she shifted the phone to her other ear.

"Are you all right? You sound a little shaky."

"Wouldn't you be if you almost got on a plane that crashed?" She pressed the receiver closer to her ear so she could hear him better, then reached for the remote and turned the volume down on the television.

"Yeah, I guess I would! Look… Are you going to be all right? Do you need some company?"

"Company?" her voice quaked with emotion as she swiped moisture from her cheek.

"Yeah, I could bring over some Chinese," he offered.

"Oh, well . . ." She didn't know what to say. She sniffed and brushed her palm to her other cheek. "I hate to put you out."

"It's no trouble. I need dinner, and I don't feel like eating alone tonight . . . thought maybe you wouldn't either."

She hesitated, then agreed, "All right. I guess."

She gave him her address and hung up the phone. Looking down at her sweats, she decided she couldn't possibly let Nick Aimes see her like this. She rummaged back through her closet and found a nice pair of jeans and a Christmas sweater that she'd picked up for herself the other day at the store.

She spent the next hour adjusting her hair and makeup and nervously flitting around the apartment making sure it was clean. At the last minute, she decided they'd need a dessert and whipped up a pecan pie and put it in the oven. Nothing like warm pecan pie with a dollop of fresh whipped cream on top!

When the doorbell rang, Elaina's stomach, which had already been twisting in nervous knots, fluttered even more. She opened the door and greeted Nick. He still had on his blue dress shirt and tie, but it was loosened at the top and he wore a leather jacket. He held the bags of Chinese food in one hand and reached out to put his other hand on her arm.

"Are you all right? I still can't believe what happened to your flight!" He stepped inside her apartment, and she motioned for him to put the Chinese food on the kitchen table.

"I'm still a little rattled." She held up her trembling hands as proof. But she wasn't so sure whether she was shaking because of her near brush with death or the fact that Nick Aimes had invited himself over to her apartment.

Nick set the bags down and took her hands in his. "It's a miracle you didn't get on that plane. What happened? Do you feel like talking about it?" He stepped closer to her, and warmth drizzled over her starting at the point of his touch.

Unaccustomed to the sensation, Elaina looked down, noting how small her hands looked in his. "Let me grab some plates, and I'll tell you about it while we eat," she suggested pulling away from him and turning toward the cupboards. She got them some sodas, plates and forks, and they sat down at the table.

"You mind if we say a prayer?" Nick pointed to the food. She nodded. He blessed the food and thanked God for keeping Elaina safe and for sparing her life. He also prayed for all the people who lost family and friends on the flight.

As Nick concluded his prayer, Elaina heard her mother's voice, *"There are people that you are supposed to love that you aren't loving."* Was Nick one of those people? He sure seemed like someone her parents would have chosen for her! He was completely different than anyone she would have selected for herself only a few days prior! Four days ago, she would have laughed him out of the building if he'd suggested that he bring dinner over to her apartment, much less offer a prayer!

"So, tell me how you managed to miss that flight," Nick prompted, leaning his elbow on the table.

"I was late, as you know – you saw me. And then when I was on my way out to the car, a little girl stopped me and asked me to help her find her mother. There was no one else around to help her, so I had no choice. She wouldn't get in my car, so we had to walk several blocks, and then she wouldn't let me leave her until her mother arrived. Her mother was out scouring the streets for her."

"So a good deed saved your life," Nick smiled.

"That little girl saved my life!" Elaina corrected him. "What if she hadn't gotten lost? I'd be dead right now."

"What if you hadn't been kind enough to help her?" Nick pointed out.

Elaina shrugged, a little embarrassed.

Nick's eyes squinted as he looked at her with a puzzled smile, "What's gotten into you, Elaina Houston? You're not the same person you were a few days ago."

"You mean I'm not the Ice Woman anymore?" she raised a single eyebrow.

Nick turned a little red, "Now, I know you've never heard me call you that."

"No, but I know other people do."

"They wouldn't call you Ice Woman now. What's caused this sudden change?" His eyes met hers and she sensed a connection with him that she had never felt with anyone else.

She wanted to tell him. If anyone would believe her, Nick would. However, she still wasn't ready to open up to him with the full story. A bit unnerved by her attraction to him, she looked down, letting her finger trace a circle on the tabletop as she tried to think of an answer that would satisfy him. "Let's just say that I don't hate God anymore for what happened to my parents, and I've decided to start living my life like they would've wanted me to."

"Oh," Nick's eyebrows rose and then he nodded with understanding. "I guess it was rough losing both of your parents. Would it be too forward of me to ask how it happened?"

Elaina took a deep breath and released a long slow exhale. "They died in a car crash on Christmas Eve – when I was twelve."

"Mmm," Nick sympathized with a shake of his head.

"As you can imagine, I've never been too fond of Christmas since," she glanced at him with a weak smile. She expected to find pity in his eyes, but instead she saw warmth and understanding. Again, a sensation of connection passed between them for several silent moments.

He finally spoke, "So what changed it for you this year? What made you decide to stop blaming God for what happened?"

Again, she felt the urge to confide in him. He engendered such trust, but she couldn't bring herself to tell him what had happened. "Please don't take this the wrong way, Nick. But it's kind of personal, and I'd really rather not talk about it."

"Fair enough," he put up a hand of surrender, "I'm sorry. I shouldn't pry."

She reached for his hand. "You're not prying." Her eyes met his, pleading with him for a little more time. "It's just sort of a – I guess you could say a sacred experience for me, and I'm not ready to talk about it yet." She paused, hoping he would understand, "Maybe someday."

He covered her hand with his and his blue eyes held hers for several moments. Elaina wondered if the expression on Nick's face meant he felt the same stirring of emotion she did.

Clearing his throat, Nick lifted his nose and inhaled, "Something sure smells good all of a sudden."

"Oh, I put a pie in the oven for our dessert," she smiled.

"Pecan?"

"Yep," her head bobbed.

"My favorite!"

"Really? Mine too. Of course, I'm a dessert-aholic though. I used to love desserts so much that my parents called me Puddin'."

"Cute. My parents called me Stinker," Nick confided.

"Stinker?" she chuckled

"Yeah, I used to have a little problem with foot odor," he whispered.

"Then please do keep your shoes on while you're here," she teased.

"I don't have the problem anymore. I finally learned to change my socks on a daily basis," he laughed.

"That does help!"

Nick and Elaina spent the next hour eating and getting to know each other on a more personal level. Nick told her about his family, and Elaina told him about her brothers and their families who were both very religious. She even found herself opening up to him about her life and why she'd shut out the world. She thought it would be easier to close herself off, but realized now that she'd just made things more difficult for herself.

"I really need to call my brothers, but I'm just not sure where to start with them. I can't just call them up and say I've changed. They'd never believe me. You can't just talk about change; you have to prove it by your actions."

"You want me to talk to them with you? I can be your witness – you know of your change of heart!" he chuckled half-teasing and half-serious.

"I think I need to plan some visits with them. I'm thinking of calling my brother in Morristown first and see if I can drive up there on one of my vacation days after Christmas."

"That's a good idea." Nick nodded.

The timer rang. Elaina stood up, crossed the kitchen, and slipped on two oven mitts. She pulled the pie from the oven and set it on a rack. "It'll have to cool a while before we can eat it. Feel like watching a movie or something?" she asked as she removed the mitts and set them on the counter.

"Sure, whatcha got?"

"I picked up some Christmas movies the other day at the store. Figured I need to make up for lost time," she laughed. "They're right over there. Pick one out while I make some whipped cream for the pie."

Nick selected "Miracle on 34th Street," and started it. Elaina put the whipped cream in the refrigerator and sat a fair distance from Nick on the couch. She wasn't sure whether he was just trying to be her friend or whether he wanted something more. So keeping her distance, she decided, would be safer.

Twenty minutes into the movie, Nick asked if they could have some pie. The aroma was getting to him. Elaina stopped the movie and fixed two plates. When she returned, Nick had scooted over to the center of the couch. No matter which side she chose, she was going to be close to him. She handed him a plate and sat down on his right.

Elaina re-started the movie and after a single bite, Nick began raving about the excellence of her pie and how it was the best he'd ever tasted. She thanked him and giggled at the theatrical way he kept going on and on about how scrumptious it was.

"Now you're just being silly," she laughed.

He turned to look at her, "No, I'm serious. It's the best thing I've ever tasted." She could have sworn he was looking at her mouth.

Nick could only think of one thing that could taste better than that pie right now and it was the soft contours of Elaina's lips. He decided not to press his luck though. She'd agreed to let him come over for dinner. That didn't mean she was interested in him as anything more than a friend. She'd made enough headway in the last few days, and he figured kissing her would probably be pushing it. But she was looking at his lips.

No, better not, he decided and turned his gaze back to the television. He set the empty pie plate on a magazine atop the coffee table and reached his right arm out along the back of the couch.

He felt like he was in junior high trying to get his arm around the prettiest girl in school. She set her empty pie plate on his, and when she leaned back she moved a little closer to him. He took her signal and eased his arm around her shoulder. She snuggled up next to him and put her feet up on the coffee table. Nick enjoyed the rest of the movie with her next to him. She felt right there, and he still couldn't shake the sheer wonder of what was happening.

"Thanks for bringing over the Chinese. I enjoyed the company," Elaina smiled as she accompanied Nick to the door.

"Thanks for the pie and the movie," he reached out to enfold her in a hug. She put her arms around his waist and hugged him. He wondered when had been the last time anyone had given her a hug. Knowing her need for human connection, he held her in his arms until she leaned back and smiled at him.

"Merry Christmas, Elaina," he winked with a grin.

"Merry Christmas, Nick."

He leaned over and gave her a friendly peck on the lips, and the next thing he knew, Elaina's arms were around his neck, and she was kissing him. Actually he was kissing her. He wasn't sure who started it. It was more of a simultaneous, mutual decision. And he was right. She did taste even better than the pie! He needed to leave, but he wanted to hold her a little longer, kiss her a little more.

Using some restraint, he broke their affections and hugged her one more time. "I better go," he whispered into her ear. "I'll see you in the morning."

"Good night," she replied as he opened the door and left.

Elaina made sure her door was locked and bolted, and then ran her hands through her ash-blonde locks. She grinned heavenward, "Now if he's part of your plan for me, then I think I'm going to like this."

December 21st

Elaina tried not to let the fact that one more encounter with death lay ahead of her, and there were still several more days until Christmas Eve. She tried to focus on helping others and reaching outside of herself when she really felt like hiding in her apartment until the twenty-fifth.

The one thing that made her want to venture out was Nick. She could hardly eat her breakfast she was so excited and nervous to see him again. It could get awkward at work.

When she reached her office, Angela handed her an envelope, "This came for you this morning."

"What is it?" Elaina asked as she took it.

"I don't know."

"Who left it?"

"Don't know that either," Angela shrugged.

Elaina ripped open the sealed envelope with her name on it. Inside she found a card and a ticket to the Opera. The card read, *"I've got the matching ticket. Care to join me? If so, I'll pick you up at seven. Love, Nick."*

Love? Was that a casual closing or did he mean something by that?

"Must be something good," Angela commented on the broad smile across her boss' face.

"It's a ticket to the opera for tomorrow night," she tried to wipe the dreamy look off her face.

"Wow, I hope someone else has the other ticket and you aren't expected to go alone."

"No, I won't be going alone," she grinned and carried the card and ticket into her office, leaving Angela's curiosity unsatisfied.

Elaina had a hard time concentrating because she kept thinking about Nick, but she forced herself to work. Around one o'clock she received an instant message from him.

"So are we on for tomorrow night?" Nick asked.

"Sounds great, thanks for asking," she replied.

"You're welcome. I had fun last night, by the way."

"Me too. Thanks for bringing dinner over."

"Do you like Italian?" he inquired.

"Love it."

"Great! Do you think you'll have any of that delicious pecan pie left by tomorrow night?"

"Sure, and if not, I'll make another one."

"Then let's save some room for dessert," he replied.

Elaina pictured Nick coming to her apartment for dessert. She smiled, remembering the flavor of his kiss. "You don't have to keep making a big deal out of my pecan pie. I know you're just being nice," she typed.

"You're right. It's really only the second best thing I've ever tasted."

"Aha! So now the truth comes out! Tell me… what's the first?"

"You."

Elaina put her hands to her cheeks to cool them. How could a man make her blush without even being in the room with her? She couldn't think of a reply to top his so she typed a blushing smiley face symbol and told him she better get back to work.

This very type of thing had been one reason why she'd hidden her heart for so many years. Now she was useless! All she could think about was Nick and the way it felt to kiss him and feel his arms around her. She began to wonder if Nick were part of God's plan or simply something to throw her off track – a test to see if she'd trip up and miss some small and simple thing that could cost her life. But, it felt so right to be with him! She hoped and prayed that she'd make it to Christmas, because life was looking better than it ever had before.

December 22nd

"Got any pie left?" Nick instant messaged her the next morning.

"I got the munchies and ate the rest of it last night."

"Darn, well I'll just have to have some of my favorite dessert instead," he teased.

"There's plenty of that, but if you get bored with it, I made a citrus cheesecake this morning," she typed.

"Not going to get bored with it. I can assure you, but thanks for making a citrus cheesecake for me! Sounds delicious!"

"Are you kidding? I made it for myself! They didn't call me Puddin' for nothing!"

"All right... put that beautiful nose to the grindstone, Puddin', and I'll see you tonight at seven."

A broad grin lifting Elaina's cheeks. "Can't wait!" she typed.

Elaina was so wrapped up in her blooming relationship with Nick that she almost forgot that she might not live to see another Christmas day. Her Christmas guest list had grown significantly. She'd invited Darryl the doorman, Janet from work who had no family nearby, and the lady in the next apartment down who also planned to spend Christmas alone. If she'd given in to her selfish desires, she would have told everyone the dinner was off and spent it alone with Nick, but she knew that wasn't the right thing to do. Besides, he hadn't said for sure whether he planned to be there.

She put on her best evening gown, swept her hair up in an elegant style and wore her fur coat. She'd splurged and bought it a couple years earlier.

Nick arrived promptly at seven and whistled when she opened the door.

"My word, Elaina! You're gorgeous," he leaned over to kiss her cheek lightly.

"Thank you," she smiled as she gathered her purse and locked up.

"My Explorer might be a little clunky for you in that gown. Do you want to take your car instead?"

"That's okay, I can manage it," she accompanied him down the staircase. "I still haven't gotten my car back from the shop."

They left the building and entered the parking lot. He opened the car door for her and she was stunned when he lifted her off the ground and set her inside the Explorer.

The night was perfect, just as she knew it would be – a romantic dinner at a quaint Italian restaurant, an evening at the opera, and Nick coming up to her apartment for a piece of citrus cheesecake.

"Make yourself at home. I've got to get out of this dress before I fix any whipped cream," she went back to her bedroom and shut the door.

Nick opened the refrigerator which was stocked with ingredients for Christmas day. Finding the cheesecake and a carton of whipping cream, he pulled both of them out and set them on the counter. He crossed to the living room and began thumbing through Elaina's music and movies.

"Ah, now this feels a million times better," she sighed as she emerged from her room in a pair of jeans and a sweater. She went to the kitchen to whip up some topping.

"What are you doing Christmas Eve?" Nick asked once they sat down at the kitchen table.

"I guess I'll be cooking a lot of food," she smiled.

"Looks like you have a fridge full, that's for sure!"

"So have you decided if you'll be joining us for Christmas day?" She cut into a piece of cheesecake.

"Us?" his quizzical eyes narrowed.

"I invited a few other people from the neighborhood and Janet from work. I even called my brother Chuck last night and invited his family. He said they'd be here."

"Wow, how many people is that?"

"Let's see…" Elaina started counting on her fingers. Eleven not counting me; twelve if you can make it," she replied and then added, "Will you be here?"

"If you have room, I'd love to come."

"There's always room for you," she winked.

"Need some help cooking on Friday?" He leaned his elbow on the table.

"Are you a good cook?"

"Not really, but I'm an excellent taste tester, and I could hand you the ingredients," he chuckled, and then took a bite of cheesecake.

"Every chef needs a good taste tester," she winked.

Nick ate the last of his cheesecake, complimented her on the dessert and rose from his seat, "It's late. I better let you get some rest for work tomorrow."

Elaina followed him to the door, "Thanks, Nick. I had a great time."

"Me too." He put his palm to her cheek, stroking the softness of her skin with his thumb. She was beautiful, and he couldn't believe she'd been right under his nose all this time. He'd never realized what a remarkable person she was inside. He'd been blind. On the other hand, maybe she had been hidden all that time.

Again he wanted to ask her what had brought her out of her shell. Instead he kissed her, gently at first and then he sensed that she needed something more from him. She needed to be held, to be loved by someone who wouldn't take advantage of her, but would give her the affection she hadn't had in far too long.

With one bold gesture, he swept her up into his arms and carried her to the couch. There was a deep, dark, empty space in Elaina's heart that she hadn't realized existed until this moment and just as she became aware of it, Nick filled it. With every touch of his lips to hers, every stroke of her hair, every embrace, love filled the vacancy in her heart. She wondered how she could have existed all these years without being aware of the vacuum within her soul.

Nick seemed to sense her needs. He stopped kissing her and just held her, letting her nuzzle her head against his chest, her arms wrapped around him. There was a security in his embrace that made her forget the past, healed her loss and assured her that somehow, someway she would survive to see many more Christmases to come. Hopefully all of them would be spent just like this one – in Nick's arms.

December 23rd

The last day of work before Christmas at Mullins and Mullrooney was always a festive occasion of Christmas bonuses and the company party. This year was no different and it was the first time Nick and Elaina had a chance to be together in a more relaxed setting at work.

She wondered how they should act toward each other. She'd managed to keep the fact that she had been dating Nick from her secretary and staff, and she kind of liked it that way. She liked keeping him to herself. On the other hand, after last night all she wanted to do was hover by his side, hold his hand, and claim him as her own for all to see.

She decided to play it by ear – follow his lead. If he felt comfortable being seen with Ice Woman, then that would tell her something, wouldn't it?

The office party started at three and she'd only received one instant message from Nick earlier that morning saying he'd be in meetings up until the time of the party. She worked until the time came, shut down her computer and left her office.

As Elaina closed her office door, she asked, "Are you ready for the Christmas party, Angela?"

"Yeah, I'll be there in a little bit. I just need to file a few more things," Angela crossed to the filing cabinet with an armful of manila folders.

Elaina waited for her and then the two of them went to the employee break room. It had been decorated with a Christmas tree, garland and lights. The table was laden with festive food and treats spread out on a green and red holiday tablecloth. Mullins and Mullrooney always hired the best catering company in town for their Christmas party.

Mr. Mullins greeted Elaina at the door with a smile and a hug, "I'm so happy we overbooked you Monday and you didn't get on that plane! I feel just awful that I could have sent you to your death!"

"It's all right, Mr. Mullins. I think I had a couple of guardian angels looking out for me," she smiled.

"And let's hope they keep looking out for you. You're making some excellent progress in your department! We couldn't do business without you."

"Thank you," she smiled at her employer.

"Isn't that right, Roger?" Mr. Mullins turned to his partner.

"That's right, Elaina. You're doing a fantastic job. And so is my boy, Nick!" The elderly gentleman pointed to Nick who had just entered the room. "Over here, Nick" he motioned for Nick to join them.

Elaina could feel her pulse quicken at the mere mention of his name. She wasn't even sure when he'd left last night. She'd fallen asleep on his shoulder. He must have carried her to bed and slipped out. When she woke that morning, she could smell the scent of him on her clothes. She almost wore the same sweater to work so she could keep his scent with her, but figured someone else might notice it too.

The familiar fragrance of his cologne filled her senses, and she closed her eyes for a second and inhaled. She didn't know if she could look at him without giving away her infatuation for him, so she kept smiling at Mr. Mullrooney.

"You two make a great team!" Mullrooney slapped Nick on the shoulder.

"It's amazing what you two can accomplish when you put your heads together!" Mullins added and Elaina could feel the crimson rising to her cheeks. He wouldn't be saying that if he knew just how much they'd put their heads together!

"Those ideas you two came up with for the Gilberts were fantastic. They loved them and the market testing looks very encouraging!" Mullrooney added.

"Thank you, Sir," they answered in unison.

Nick must have sensed her embarrassment and put his palm to the center of her back. She supposed he did it for support, but it just sent her emotions bouncing in all directions.

"Are you all right, Elaina? You look a little flushed," Mr. Mullins noted.

"I'm fine. I'm just a little warm with this turtleneck, I guess." She gave her collar a nervous tug.

"I'll get you some punch," Nick offered and headed for the buffet table.

"If you'll excuse me, Elaina, I'm going to catch Fred before he has to leave," Mullins pointed across the room and Mullrooney excused himself as well.

Nick returned with two cups of punch and handed her one, "You know, I think Mr. Mullins is right, we need to put our heads together more often."

Elaina nearly choked on her sip of punch.

"I think the copy room is empty," he teased with a wink.

"You're awful," she rolled her eyes.

"I know," he winked.

"Thanks for last night," she smiled.

"Sure, anytime," he kept looking at her with a flirtatious grin. She hoped his feelings for her weren't as obvious to everyone else as they were to her.

~*~

"So what's going on between you and Nick?" Janet asked as she stepped into the ladies room. Elaina dried her hands on a paper towel.

"What do you mean?" Elaina tried to play it cool, but she could feel her lips drawing into a silly grin like the one Nick had been wearing.

"It's obvious you two have a thing for each other," Janet observed as she brushed her long black hair and stared at her reflection in the mirror.

"We do not have a 'thing'," Elaina rolled her eyes.

"Yes you do," Janet insisted.

"Okay, so we've been dating a little," Elaina confided.

"Will he be at your Christmas dinner?"

"Yes."

"Then you definitely have a thing."

"I guess it all depends on what your definition of 'a thing' is." A sly grin lifted Elaina's lips and she reached for the door.

"Oh, what time do you want me at your place on Saturday?" Janet called out as Elaina started out of the restroom.

"Be there around six."

"Okay."

Elaina turned the corner and almost ran into Nick as he came down the hall.

"Oh, I'm sorry," she apologized.

He leaned his hand against the wall, blocking her path, "Run into me anytime."

Elaina looked around to make sure no one else saw them flirting in the hallway. Noting that they were alone, she leaned her shoulder against the wall facing him.

"What are you doing tonight?" he asked.

"Just puttering around, getting a few things done."

"Care if I stop by for a little while? I have something I'd like to bring over."

"Oh really? What?"

"No, it's a surprise," he winked.

"I don't know if I like surprises," Elaina's fingers fiddled with Nick's tie.

"You'll like this one," he smiled.

"Break it up you two," Jeff Richards slapped Nick on the back as he passed them and turned the corner.

"Let's get out of here," Nick extended his hand to Elaina.

"I need to get a few things from my office."

"Okay, meet me back here at the elevator.

~*~

Once the doors of the elevator shut, Nick stepped closer to Elaina and put his hands on her waist. She knew that look in his eye.

"Oh, come on Nick," she chuckled. "Not in the office elevator."

"But there's mistletoe," he pointed upward where someone had used a red ribbon to hang a sprig of mistletoe from the ceiling.

She looked up at it and then into his pale blue eyes. A mischievous grin captured his expression, and he took her in his arms and kissed her from the fifteenth floor all the way down to the first. Fortunately, the elevator made the trip down without interruption.

By the time the door opened, she'd grown weak in the knees from what only could be described as the most toe-tingling, ankle-raising, mind-boggling, heart-stopping, take-your-breath-away-and-make-you-forget-to-breathe kiss she'd ever received in her twenty-four years of living.

Wow was the only thing that entered her mind. Every other coherent thought had fled.

Nick took her hand, led her out of the building and to her rental car.

"I've got to go pick up that surprise," he kissed her cheek and helped her into the car. "When do you want me to stop by?"

"Oh," her brain was still mush from the elevator ride, but she pulled her thoughts together, "How about around six? I'll make you some of my world famous pecan chicken," her dimples deepened, her face aglow.

"You've got a deal," he shut her door. She backed out of the parking spot, waved goodbye and drove away.

~*~

Around six, the buzzer rang and Elaina let Nick into the building. After a few minutes she heard *Thud, Swish, Thud, Swish, Thud, Swish, Thud, Swish Swish* out in the hallway.

Curious, she opened her door and found Nick dragging a six foot Christmas tree behind him, a white plastic bag hanging from his wrist and a tree stand in his hand.

"Merry Christmas!" he greeted, a little breathless. His eyes twinkled and his cheeks were pink from being out in the cold air.

"You brought me a Christmas tree!" she exclaimed, opening the door wider.

"Well, you can't celebrate Christmas without a tree," he insisted as he pulled the tree inside.

"I guess you're right about that," she said as she grabbed the bag and the tree stand from him so that he could use both hands to bring the tree further into the apartment.

"Where should we put it?" he asked.

She pointed. "What about over here in the corner? I can move this table."

"Great idea," he agreed and she shut the door.

"I thought we could put the lights on tonight, and I'll come back tomorrow and we can shop for ornaments and decorate it then. I figure a woman wants to select her own ornaments," he dragged the tree over to the corner Elaina had indicated. Soon Nick had the tree standing upright.

They ate dinner and trimmed the tree. Nick strung the lights while Elaina sat on the couch watching him and listening to Christmas music.

"My aunt Vicky always used to say that the number one criteria in a husband is that he be willing to string Christmas lights," Elaina chuckled, tucking her hands behind her head as she leaned back watching him.

"And are you husband-hunting?" Nick raised an eyebrow.

"Oh, I didn't mean to imply anything by that," Elaina blushed, bringing her hands back to her lap. "I had just forgotten that she used to say it until I sat here watching you string those lights."

"So I'd pass with Aunt Vicky's approval then?" He put his hands in his pockets and turned toward her.

"I guess so, I guess you would," she stammered, embarrassed by what her remark implicated.

"Good. One relative down, now to see if I pass inspection with your brother." He winked and went back to his light stringing.

Elaina couldn't believe how Nick had reacted to her remark. Most men would have left skid marks at even the remotest insinuation of marriage. But Nick acted as if the obvious culmination of their relationship would lead to the altar. They'd only been dating for a few days!

Was she doing the right thing with Nick? What if she didn't pass the last test? The last few days without incident had given her a false sense of security. She'd been so wrapped up in Nick and enjoying the season that she'd almost forgotten that death hung around the corner. Would it be today? Tomorrow? That's all there was left.

"What's wrong, Elaina?" Nick stopped fiddling with the lights and his concerned eyes met hers.

"Huh? Oh nothing," she shook her head, and did her best to force the frown into a pleasant expression, but she wasn't having much success.

"You've got a dark cloud over your head all of a sudden," he noted and stepped toward her. "And I know just the thing to chase it away."

He pushed her coffee table to the side, picked up the remote control and changed from the holiday channel to one playing love songs.

"May I have this dance?" He took a deep bow.

She laughed and he took her hand, helping her to her feet. He held her in a traditional pose for several moments until she slipped both her hands around his neck and his went around her waist.

Elaina leaned her head against his shoulder and brushed a tear from her eyes.

"Are you crying?" he whispered. "Won't you tell me what's wrong so I can help?"

"I can't – not yet," she shook her head and closed her eyes.

"Isn't there something I can do?" he grimaced. He pressed his hand to her cheek and brushed away a tear.

"Just hold me. You have no idea how much that helps," she hugged him tighter and he gave her the consolation she so desperately needed.

December 24th

"Come on up here and have some hot cocoa!" Elaina called down into the alley to Roberta and her 14-year-old son, Hakeem.

"That's okay, Ms. Houston," the woman shook her head.

"Nonsense, get up here. I made way too much. It's homemade and it smells delicious!"

"Come on, Mom, I'm freezing," Hakeem pleaded.

"See there, come on up," Elaina waved.

The buzzer rang and Elaina let the mother and son into her apartment.

Elaina set two steaming cups of cocoa on her kitchen table and motioned for them to sit. "I've got some cheesecake too…. That is if Nick didn't eat it all," she peered into the refrigerator rummaging for any leftover dessert.

"Yes, here it is," she pulled it out, cut them each a piece, and sat down with them at the table with her own cup of cocoa.

"You're too kind, Miss Houston," the woman replied and took a sip of the warm sweet liquid.

"Nonsense!" Elaina waved her hand as if it were nothing. "And please, call me Elaina."

After several minutes of small talk, Elaina had the pair opening up and confiding in her. Roberta explained that her husband had left them with a pile of debts about eighteen months earlier. Because she'd been a homemaker since high school, she had never gained the skills or education needed to obtain a decent job. Soon her car and her home were repossessed, and they were out on the streets.

She and Hakeem lived at a shelter at night, and she did odd jobs around town trying to earn a little extra money, but no one wanted to hire someone who didn't have a permanent address.

"Do you have family members anywhere that you could stay with until you get back on your feet?" Elaina suggested.

"I have a sister in St. Louis, and she said we could stay with her, but neither she nor we have the money for the trip. I'm trying to save up enough for bus tickets, but it's slow going."

"Hmmm," an idea began to percolate in Elaina's inventive mind.

The next minute, Nick was downstairs asking to come up. She rose from her chair and let him into the building.

"You have company coming, we should be on our way," Roberta stood and motioned for Hakeem to do the same.

"No, stay here. I want you to meet Nick. He'll be here for Christmas dinner tomorrow. You are still coming at six – right?"

The woman seemed surprised, "Are you sure you want us?"

"Of course, I'm sure. I'm planning on you both being here!"

Elaina let Nick in and introduced him to Roberta and Hakeem and informed him they'd be joining them for dinner the next day. Nick greeted the pair with the same friendly countenance he showed everyone he met. After they left, Elaina explained Roberta's situation to him.

Just as she concluded her retelling of Roberta's account, she started to her office. "I have an idea," she booted her computer. "I want to buy both of them plane tickets to St. Louis."

Nick interjected, "Oh, let me help!"

"Really? I didn't mean for you to..."

"No, I want to. It'll be fun. Just think of how excited they'll be tomorrow when you give them the tickets."

"When WE give them the tickets," she gave Nick a hug and sat down in front of the computer to purchase two tickets to St. Louis for Roberta and Hakeem.

~*~

Nick and Elaina spent the day shopping for decorations and putting the ornaments on the tree. They cooked pies and other side dishes that could safely be prepared the day before.

It was around six o'clock Christmas Eve when Elaina remembered she'd neglected to purchase sage for the dressing.

"I'll go get it for you," Nick offered.

"No, I think I should go. I'd like to look around the store and make sure I haven't forgotten anything. You stay here and watch the pies for me. Just take them out when the timer goes off."

"All right. Be careful," he kissed her cheek and she grabbed her purse and keys.

"I'll be right back," she waved and was gone.

Elaina grabbed the sage at the superstore and looked around for something for Nick. She'd still not found anything that said what she wanted to say with a gift. A Christmas present when you're first dating has to be chosen carefully, after all. If the gift is too flamboyant, he'll think you're pushing, but something too frivolous could give him the idea you're not interested.

Finally, when strolling through the men's department, she spotted the perfect gift – a navy and green sweater that could have had Nick's name on it. It looked so much like something he would wear. Next she headed for the electronics department to pick up a CD by one of his favorite artists. Satisfied that she'd made an appropriate purchase, she headed for the checkout counter.

Elaina grabbed her purse and bags and stepped out of the car into her apartment complex's parking garage. Still singing the Christmas carol that played on the radio, she clicked the button on her key ring to lock the door. From the darkness, she felt someone strike her arm, knocking her keys to the concrete. Fear gripped her as she drew a panicked breath. Her keys clanked noisily and fell at her feet. Elaina started to reach for them, but felt a gun lodged painfully into her side. Her assailant wrapped a scarf around her nose and mouth to muffle the sounds of her screams.

Terrified, Elaina dropped her belongings and fought back, frantic to escape.

"Get her money," a male voice barked from behind her.

She felt herself being pulled backwards and she looked down to see a familiar face rummaging through her purse, pulling the cash from her wallet. The young man looked up, his brown eyes meeting hers. He started stuffing the money back in the purse and threw it and her shopping bags together on the concrete at her feet.

"We can't rob this lady. I know her," the fourteen-year-old boy insisted, and Elaina felt a resurgence of hope, but it was short-lived.

"That doesn't matter. Our job's to rob and ice a rich white woman – this is her!" the assailant with the angry voice shoved her against the car and Elaina knew this was it – her time had come. She'd missed something and this was it. She thought of Nick and wished she had more time with him. Her stomach slammed against the vehicle, sending a searing pain through her abdomen. She could hardly breathe as the two young men stood behind her.

"She's a nice lady. We can't do this to her," she heard Hakeem pleading with the hoodlum.

"There's no such thing as a nice rich woman," the older boy pressed his body against her, holding the gun to Elaina's head. Her lungs restricted, her mind searching for some means of escape.

"It's just a stupid gang. It's not worth this!" Hakeem exclaimed.

Just then, Hakeem hurled his hand at the older boy's arm, pushing it away from Elaina. In the scuffle, the gun went off, the bullet lodging into the cinderblock wall.

"Run!" Hakeem screamed, "Run!" When Elaina turned around, Hakeem was on top of the other boy, hitting him in the face.

Elaina grabbed her bags and keys, which lay in her path toward her apartment. Her heart pounding painfully, she fled toward the entrance. When she reached the outside door, she fumbled frantically with her keys trying to find the right one, but she was too nervous to think clearly enough. She could hear footsteps approaching! They were after her!

She pressed the button and ripped the cloth from her mouth, "Nick, open up! Please, oh please! Someone's trying to kill me!"

Nick unlocked the door, and Elaina flew up the stairs as fast as she could. Nick met her halfway down. A worried scowl troubled his face.

"What's going on?" he asked.

She grabbed his hand and kept running up the stairs. "Come on, we have to get inside!" They leapt up the remaining flight and entered her apartment. Elaina slammed the door shut. She bolted it and made sure it was secure. Her sides split from her frantic escape.

"What's happened, Elaina? Talk to me! Are you all right?" he held her by the shoulders.

Elaina threw her arms around him, burying her head against his shoulder as she tried to calm down and catch her breath.

"What is it, Elaina? We need to call the police."

"No, no police," she panted. She thought of Hakeem. Would the police understand that he had protected her? What if they arrested him for his involvement? "It's over now . . . Thank heavens it's all over now!" She took a deep breath and exhaled before stepping away from Nick and pacing the floor. She kept mumbling, "It's over. It's all over now."

"What's over?"

"The death threats, that was the third one. I'm safe now."

"Death threats? What's happening, Elaina? Tell me what's going on!"

In the distance, Elaina could hear sirens wailing, growing closer.

"The police are coming. You need to talk to them," he took her hand, leading her toward the balcony. They looked out the window and watched a flashing squad car speeding toward the apartment complex.

"But I don't want to get him in trouble," she said, her face crinkling with worry.

"Who?" He took her by the shoulders, searching her eyes.

"Hakeem," she whispered, looking away from him toward the window. The squad car had disappeared into the parking garage. "A neighbor must've heard the shot," she muttered to herself.

"Hakeem? You mean that boy who came up here with his mother today?"

She nodded.

"He tried to kill you?" Elaina could see the anger rising in Nick's eyes as his protective hands tightened on her shoulders.

"No, no, he saved my life. He and another boy tried to attack me, but then Hakeem realized it was me and helped me escape. It was for some gang initiation or something."

"Stay here, I'm going for the police," he said, releasing her and marching toward the door.

"Wait, Nick!" she called after him, but he didn't stop.

Elaina put a troubled hand to her face, wondering how she could explain what happened to the police without implicating Hakeem.

It took longer than expected for Nick to return, but once he did, the officers explained they had made a sweep of the area, looking for her attackers. They had found no one.

Elaina sat at her kitchen table with Nick beside her, and the two policemen prepared to take notes across from her.

"Please tell us what happened," prompted an officer who looked like he would be someone's grandfather.

The compassionate twinkle in his eye helped her relax a little. She took a deep breath and began by explaining how she'd stepped out of her car and had her keys knocked out of her hand. "There were two of them. One attacked me from behind and the other helped me escape. They were trying to get into a gang. I was their initiation project. The one boy kept saying they were supposed to rob and ice a rich white woman. But, the other boy didn't want to do it. They struggled over the gun and it went off, but the one boy bought me some time to escape."

When the officers asked for a description, she admitted that her attacker had remained at her back the entire time. She'd never even gotten a glance at him. The one who helped her had worn a scarf. This was all true, but she didn't mention that she'd recognized Hakeem's eyes and voice. She just couldn't bring herself to involve him.

Nick gave her a stern look as if he wanted her to give more details. He didn't press her though. He respecting her decision and kept quiet about Hakeem.

After going over her story several times, the officers left Nick and Elaina alone once more. She paced to the couch and sat down, running her hands through her hair and releasing a sigh of relief.

Nick joined her, sitting sideways to look at her. "Are you going to tell me what's going on?" he prompted.

She nodded and then started at the beginning – with her parents' appearance, their warning, her quest to live a more Christ-like life, the three brushes with death, and how each of them were thwarted by the little things she'd done over the last week.

"They were just little things, Nick – things I never would have thought to do before, but they made such a huge impact on my life – on my very existence!" she concluded.

"I've never heard anything like it," he marveled.

"But you believe me – you do believe me – right?" she pleaded.

"Yes, of course, I believe you!"

She nestled into his embrace, feeling like a heavy burden had been lifted from her shoulders.

December 25th

"Come in, come in!" Nick greeted Roberta and her son Hakeem as they stepped into the apartment. Elaina ran to the door, hugged Roberta first, and then put her arms around Hakeem. He looked quite apprehensive.

"Thank you for last night," Elaina whispered into the boy's ear.

A tear formed in Hakeem's eye, "I'm so sorry, Miss Houston."

"It's okay, thank you for saving my life," she whispered as Nick led Roberta into the kitchen to taste a piece of turkey.

Elaina crossed to the tree and lifted a long narrow box wrapped in holiday paper and a red bow. "Before everyone else arrives, Nick and I would like to give you something."

"Oh, Miss Houston, you've already been so generous. We couldn't possibly take anything else from you," Roberta shook her head with a declining motion.

"It's already done, and it has your name on it so you have to take it," Elaina chuckled as she pushed the box into the woman's gloved fingers.

Roberta removed her gloves and with trembling fingers she opened the present. Her eyes stared down at the folded paper. She opened it to find two e-tickets to St. Louis.

"You can change the dates if you need to," Elaina explained.

The woman's brown eyes pooled with moisture that began to stream down her cheeks. "You both are so generous! If I didn't know better I'd say you were angels sent from heaven!"

Nick smiled at Elaina.

"Why? Why are you doing all this for us?" Roberta stammered.

"Because we want to," Elaina hugged her new friend and tears filled her eyes. Through the turkey-scented air, she heard an almost audible male voice declare, "Inasmuch as ye have done it unto one of the least of these, ye have done it unto Me."

December 2th, 4 Years Later

"Come on, Nick! We're going to be late for the airport!" Elaina fastened their baby girl into the car seat and double-checked the security of three-year-old Nicholas' seat.

Nick hurried out into the garage and bolted the door behind him. Elaina slipped into the passenger side and Nick got behind the wheel of the minivan.

"Can you believe it's been four years since we saw them last!" Elaina mused as Nick backed the car into the driveway and pressed the button to close the garage door. Christmas lights lit up the exterior of their house and snow blanketed the ground.

"Seems like yesterday," Nick marveled in agreement.

They made good time to the airport, parked the van and each parent carried a child into the terminal.

"Where did you say we'd meet them?" Nick asked, searching the sea of travelers.

"At the bottom of the escalator - just outside security."

"Do you think that's them?" Nick pointed, shifting the little boy who looked like a miniature of his father.

"I think it is!" Elaina began waving. The tall young man and his mother took a smooth ride down the escalator, each carrying a small bag on their shoulders. The man carried a long Christmas package under his arm.

"Elaina! Nick! It's so good to see you both again!" Roberta Baker threw her arms around Elaina.

"Good grief, Hakeem! You're a giant!" Nick looked up at the six-foot-six-inch handsome man and gave him a hug. "If you hadn't gotten that academic scholarship to NYU, you could've played basketball, I bet!"

"He is quite a player," his mother interjected with obvious pride. "And just look at these beautiful babies you two have! They're simply adorable!" Roberta put out her hands to take the curly blonde-headed baby girl. Elaina handed her the child.

"We're so proud of you, Hakeem! We weren't surprised when we heard you were going to be a doctor!" Nick exclaimed, patting the young man on the back.

"I never would have amounted to a thing if it hadn't been for you two. I'd probably be in jail right now, or dead," Hakeem met Elaina's eyes with his grateful chocolate brown ones.

"Oh," Elaina waved her hand as if it were nothing.

"Hakeem's right, Elaina. Who knows when or if we'd gotten off the streets. In St. Louis Hakeem and I found a new life. You know the story – my business and the wonderful school for Hakeem. We both blossomed because of you two."

"Come on now," Nick stood between their two friends and put an arm around Roberta. "You're embarrassing my wife."

Elaina halted and turned toward the pair, "I feel like I need to say something." Everyone stopped to listen to Elaina whose expression had become serious. "God changed my heart that Christmas. He gave me a small taste of the love He has for you. When you love someone like that – you want to do what you can to make things right for them. God changed my heart, and He's the one to thank because He's responsible for it all – not Nick and certainly not me. We were just … just instruments."

Roberta hugged Elaina, "We know. We're just happy that you both were willing to be those instruments."

~*~

"We're so glad you were able to stay with us for a few days," Elaina said as the car arrived in the Aimes' garage.

"You know Elaina. Always making new friends! Our Christmas dinner has turned into a yearly feast!" Nick's eyes twinkled with admiration as he glanced toward his wife.

The aroma of homemade pies and cookies filled the air as they stepped into the elegantly decorated house. A sparkling eight-foot pine stretched upward to the vaulted ceiling of the living room, decorated with angels, stars, nativity figurines and frosted gold and red balls.

Roberta let out an audible sigh at the sight of it. She dropped her bags by the door and hurried to the living room to get a better look at the tree. Her eyes scanned the house, enjoying the decorative garland and poinsettias.

"You have a beautiful home," Roberta admired.

"Thank you," Elaina smiled at the childlike wonder on her friend's face and set the baby's carrier inside the living room.

"Come on upstairs, and you can settle into your rooms," Nick motioned as little Nicholas scurried off to the kitchen for a cookie.

"Oh, but first, Hakeem, bring that package over here, please," Roberta motioned for her son to join them by the tree.

Nick followed Hakeem. Hakeem handed the package to his mother who gave it to Elaina and Nick.

"I want you to open this now."

"Before Christmas?" Nick asked.

"I'm too excited for you to have it!" Roberta motioned again for them to take the gift.

Nick held the present while Elaina pulled back the paper.

"Oh, is it one of your designs?" Elaina grew excited and glanced up at her friend.

"Did you know Mom's prints are being sold all over the country now?" Hakeem put a proud arm around his mother.

"We heard that! It's so exciting!" Elaina pulled back the paper. "So is this one of your more popular ones?" she asked before she could discern the contents.

"No. I made this one especially for you. It's an original," Roberta rubbed her hands together. "I do hope you like it."

The remaining paper dropped to the floor, and Elaina and Nick held the painting at arms length for better examination.

"It's amazing! I love it! I simply love it!" Elaina exclaimed.

"It's fantastic! What a talent you have!" Nick agreed with his wife.

"And I know just where I want to put it!" Elaina turned and pointed to a long space above the threshold to her kitchen. "Right there! Nick, don't you think it will be wonderful right there between the dining room and the kitchen so we can see it every day as a reminder?"

"Sounds perfect to me," he nodded.

"Oh, let's hang it up right this minute!" she handed the picture to Nick and hugged Roberta.

"We don't even need a ladder to do the job, because we have Hakeem!" Nick laughed as he tugged Hakeem's arm so that he would join him in hanging the picture.

In short order, the gift had been placed in its honored location, and Elaina and Nick gazed in admiration at Roberta's masterpiece.

They all looked up at the lush landscape covered with the most exquisite arrangement of flowers, trees, blossoms and roses. A garden swept from the left side of the painting to the right. The Savior's scarred palm and the cuff of his white robe entered the picture on the right. Seeds of all kinds and varieties lay scattered in his palm and spilled onto the ground. As they did so, the wind carried them in a myriad of directions.

The script in the center sent a tear trickling down Elaina's cheek:

> *"From small and simple things are*
> *great things brought to pass."*

Spread the Spirit of Christmas!

Share the e-book version of "Miss Humbug" with your friends and you'll receive a FREE audio version to listen to on your ipod, your computer or in your car!

Visit
www.MissHumbug.com
Today!

About the Author

Marnie Pehrson is the co-founder of CleanRomanceClub.com and the author of several historical fiction titles including *The Patriot Wore Petticoats, Angel and the Enemy* and *Hannah's Heart* and inspirational titles such as *You Can't Fly If You're Still Clutching the Dirt* and *Lord, Are You Sure?*

Marnie and her husband Greg are the parents of six children. She is the founder of multi-denominational SheLovesGod.com which hosts the annual SheLovesGod Virtual Women's Conference the 3rd week of October each year. Marnie has served in many capacities within her church in presidencies of the women's and children's organizations, as a Sunday school teacher, seminary teacher, and pianist.

You may also read more of her work at **http://www.MarniePehrson.com** and **http://www.CleanRomanceClub.com** . Marnie welcomes reader comments and may be reached at **marnie@marniepehrson.com** or by calling 706-866-2295.

Marnie's Other Books

Angel and the Enemy
Historical fiction, 288 pages, paperback
ISBN 0-9729750-9-8
The War between the States is raging and Angelina Stone's world is falling apart. Her beloved father lies rotting in a Union prison and when her Georgia home is invaded by Yankee officers, Angelina knows she will never be the same again.

Will Angelina be able to overcome her fears, lay prejudice aside, and learn to trust? When the stakes are high, will she risk losing everything? Only by doing so can she face the demons of her past and win the battle that rages in her own heart - a heart that is eternally tethered to . . . the enemy.

The Patriot Wore Petticoats
Historical fiction, 224 pages, paperback
ISBN: 0-9729750-4-7
Daring "Dicey" Langston, the bold and reckless rider and expert shot, saves her family and an entire village during the American Revolution. Having faced British soldiers, rushing swollen rivers, the "Bloody Scouts," and the barrel of a loaded pistol, nothing had quite prepared this valiant heroine for the heart-pounding exhilaration she'd find in the arms of one brave Patriot. Based on a true story about the author's fourth great-grandmother. Learn more at www.DiceyLangston.com

Beyond the Waterfall
Historical Fiction, 136 pages, paperback
ISBN: 0-9729750-7-1
Jillian's feet were precariously planted in two worlds: the Cherokee nation on the brink of extermination, and the world where Jesse Whitmore belonged. On her first meeting with him, the charming and handsome merchant had set her young heart ablaze. Yet, could she trust him? Or was he just like all the other white men she'd encountered? Would he stand beside her while she witnessed her nation ripped apart, or would he join the ranks of the powerful greedy to betray her? Based on family history and local legend.

Hannah's Heart
Historical Fiction, 162 pages, paperback,
ISBN: 1-59936-012-8
Hannah Jamison is ready to give her heart away. Unfortunately, the man she's falling for shows no indication of ever reciprocating her feelings. When Mother Nature intervenes in her behalf, all Hannah's dreams seem to be coming true . . . until she discovers that following her heart means losing the ones she loves. Is Hannah willing to pay the price?

Rebecca's Reveries

Historical Fiction, 224 pages, paperback,
ISBN: 0-9729750-2-0
Rebecca Marchant had led a sheltered life until she found herself inexplicably drawn to the home of her father's youth. Surrounded by the historical landscape of the Chickamauga Battlefield in Georgia, Rebecca finds herself plagued by haunting dreams and vivid visions of Civil War events. As Rebecca walks a mile in another girl's moccasins through her visions and dreams she learns about compassion, forgiveness, temptation and the power of true love.

You Can't Fly If You're Still Clutching the Dirt: How to Stop Worrying and Achieve Your God-given Potential

Inspirational Nonfiction, 148 pages, Paperback
ISBN 0-9729750-8-X
Deep down, you know God created you for a reason. He's told you that you're a child of God. You're made in His image, and He has a plan for you. You sense in your heart of hearts that you have wings to fly, but worries, fears, and insecurities drag you down to earth, preventing you from spreading your wings and taking flight.

This book will teach you how to quit worrying and trust God; easily distinguish between what you control and what God controls; find freedom to focus on the two decisions that are yours to make – What you want and Why you want it. Find deliverance from the worry-inducing questions of Who? When? How? and Where?

Lord, Are You Sure?
Inspirational, 152 pages, Paperback,
ISBN 0-9729750-0-4
A roadmap for understanding how Heavenly
Father works in your life, helping you understand
why certain problems keep repeating themselves,
how to break the cycle and unlock the mystery of
why you encounter challenges and roadblocks on
roads you felt inspired to travel.

Packets of Sunlight for Parents
Compiled by: Marnie L. Pehrson
Inspirational, 144 pages, ISBN 0-9676162-4-7
Brighten your day with inspiration for parents of
tots to teens! Inspirational quote book.

Packets of Sunlight for American Patriots
Compiled by: Marnie L. Pehrson
Inspirational, 108 pages, ISBN 0-9676162-3-9
Let the founding fathers reignite your love for free-
dom! Inspirational quote book.

10 Steps to Fulfilling Your Divine Destiny:
A Christian Woman's Guide to
Learning & Living God's Plan for Her
Inspirational, 124 pages, Paperback,
 ISBN 0-9676162-1-2
Have you ever said to yourself, "I'd love to do
great things with my life, but I'm just too busy,
too untalented, too ordinary, too afraid, too anything but extraordinary"? Inside this book you'll
learn how to reach your full God-given potential.

A Closer Walk with Him
SheLovesGod Study Lessons Volume 1
Inspiraitonal, 212 pages, paperback,
ISBN 0-9729750-3-9
A collection of insights and ponderings on the scriptures and how we can apply them to our everyday lives. Great for the faith-lift you need in the morning, just before bed, or whenever you need a quick boost of inspiration. Each lesson is self-contained and independent. Read them in any order the Spirit moves you or read the 52 lessons in order as a yearly study guide - it's up to you.

**To order call 800-524-2307 or visit
www.MarniePehrson.com**

www.ingramcontent.com/pod-product-compliance
Lightning Source LLC
Chambersburg PA
CBHW020140150626
46552CB00021B/849